Copyright © 2003 by Nord–Süd Verlag AG, Gossau Zürich, Switzerland
First published in Switzerland under the title *Axel und Bibi*.
English translation copyright © 2003 by North–South Books Inc., New York

First published in the United States, Great Britain, Canada, Australia,
and New Zealand in 2003 by North–South Books, an imprint
of Nord–Süd Verlag AG, Gossau Zürich, Switzerland.

Distributed in the United States by North–South Books Inc., New York.

Library of Congress Cataloging–in–Publication Data is available.
A CIP catalogue record for this book is available from The British Library.

ISBN 0-7358-1797-9 (trade edition)
1 3 5 7 9 HC 10 8 6 4 2
ISBN 0-7358-1798-7 (library edition)
1 3 5 7 9 LE 10 8 6 4 2

Printed in Belgium

For more information about our books, and the authors and artists
who create them, visit our web site: www.northsouth.com

Rufus and Max

BY Hermann Moers

ILLUSTRATED BY Philippe Goossens

Translated by Kathryn Grell

North-South Books

New York / London

Rufus and Max were best friends. They lived in a small, wooden doghouse and spent every day together romping and playing in the meadow. One morning, though, they couldn't decide what to play.

"How about hide-and-seek?" Rufus suggested.

"We played hide-and-seek yesterday," said Max. "I want to do something different."

Rufus scrunched his nose in thought, and then said, "Why don't we build a castle? That way, we could be kings of the entire meadow."

"A castle!" exclaimed Max. "That sounds like fun!"

The two dogs busily set to work.

They built a castle with tall towers, many windows, and wide doors–everything they thought a good castle should have.

"It looks wonderful," said Max proudly.

"I can't wait to show our friends."

Donkey was the first guest to arrive.

"What do you think?" asked Rufus and Max excitedly. "Isn't it the most beautiful castle you have ever seen?"

Donkey looked carefully at the castle and said, "It's nice, but I almost walked right over the door. You should build a porch so everyone knows where to enter."

"Of course! A porch!" said Max. "Why didn't we think of that?"

As Donkey trotted away, Rufus and Max dragged two long planks of wood to the front of the castle. They decorated their new porch with fresh flowers.

"Now that everyone knows this is the front door, they will be sure to come and visit," said Max.

They waited, but no one came.

"Maybe the porch is too small," said Rufus. "We should build a bigger one. Let's ask Beaver to chop down the tallest tree in the forest for us."

Beaver was glad to help and soon he had gnawed down a huge tree. But as hard as Rufus and Max pushed and pulled, the fallen tree would not budge.

"This is impossible," Max panted. "There must be another way to make our castle stand out."

"Why don't we ask Fox?" suggested Rufus. "He's always full of ideas."

Rufus and Max thanked Beaver for his help and then walked deeper into the forest to search for Fox.

They found him lying under a tree. "Of course I can help," said Fox, yawning. "But my advice is not cheap. It will cost you one basket of eggs and a bag of nuts."

Rufus and Max were anxious to hear his plan, so they agreed.

"What you need," Fox said, "is a sign with your castle's name on it. Everyone will notice it then."

"Rufus, that's *exactly* what our castle is missing!" cried Max.

They both ran back to make the sign.

But even the bold letters on the sign did not catch the other animals' attention. Two rabbits scampered right through the middle of the castle, a goat tramped across all of the doors, and a pig almost crushed the north tower.

"Why doesn't anyone see our new house?" wailed Max.

Goose and Turkey, who were walking by, stopped in surprise. "Your new house?" repeated Goose. "I didn't even know you had moved!"

"You should put up a flag with directions on it," said Turkey. "That way everyone will know that you don't live in the doghouse anymore."

"What a great idea," said Max. "Thank you!"

Rufus grabbed a pillowcase from the clothesline and made the flag. "Everyone will surely come now!" he said.

Both dogs waited, but still no one came.

In frustration, Rufus and Max tore down the sign and the flag.

"Forget it," Rufus growled. "We don't need them to have fun. We can be kings by ourselves."

BEST CASTLE EVER

WE'VE MOVED ←

So they dressed up in their finest clothes and paraded regally around the castle.

Suddenly, Rufus stopped. "Wait!" he said. "We're not true kings. We don't have crowns!"

"You're right," said Max. "But where would we get those?"

"Let's search the forest and see what we can find," said Rufus.

Max dug up a rusty nail, and Rufus
saw an old shoe, but neither one found
anything that would make a good crown.
"Oh well," said Max cheerfully, "let's go
back to the castle."

When they got there, they had
quite a shock. Cat, Horse, and Cow
were having
a picnic
on top of
their castle!
"What are
you doing?"
cried Rufus.
"You're eating
lunch on our house!"

"You've covered up
our beautiful porch and you're getting
crumbs in our windows!" shouted Max.

The other animals stared at them in surprise.
"I don't know what you're talking about,"
said Cow. "We just sat down to have a picnic."

"I don't see a house anywhere," said
Cat looking around.

"I think you're being very foolish," muttered
Horse, and went back to eating his oats.

Max flopped down on the ground, dejected. "Maybe they're right," he said to Rufus. "This is just a silly game. After all, there really *isn't* a castle and we really *aren't* kings."

"Says who?" demanded Rufus defiantly. "I don't care if no one else can see our castle, I've certainly felt like a king all day. Look!" he said, running into the garden. "Here are our guards, tall and proud, all lined up at attention."

Rufus dashed back to the castle. "And here!" he said, gesturing at the creatures on the ground. "Our royal subjects, all ready to serve us."

Max laughed. Rufus's enthusiasm was endless. "You are quite right, Your Highness," Max said, bowing deeply. "We clearly are kings of the meadow!"

The two dogs spent the rest of the afternoon playing in their castle. But when it started to get dark, both agreed that they missed their snug little doghouse. It was time to go home.

The next morning, Rufus and Max woke up
early and bounded off down the road. Who knew
where their imagination would take them today!